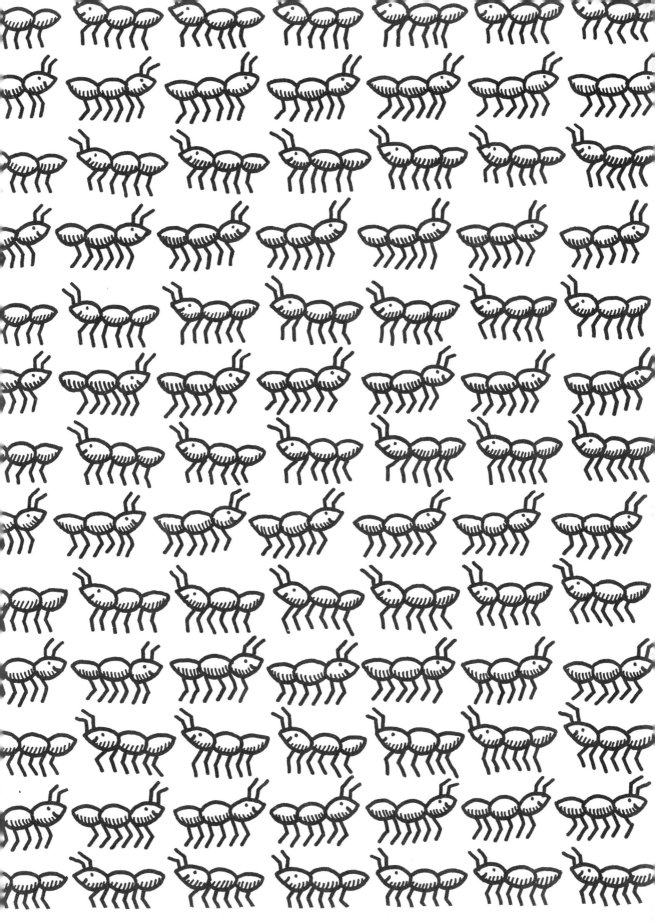

THERE'S AN ANT IN ANTHONY

BY BERNARD MOST

MULBERRY BOOKS, New York

Library of Congress Cataloging in Publication Data

Most, Bernard.   There's an ant in Anthony.

Summary: After discovering an "ant" in his own name, Anthony searches for the word "ant" in other words.
[1. Vocabulary—Fiction] I. Title.
PZ7.M8544Th   [E]   79-23089
ISBN 0-688-11513-6

Printed in the United States of America.
10 9 8 7 6 5 4 3 2

First Mulberry Edition, 1992.

To Amy with love,
for all your help.

Anthony was learning
how to spell his name in school one day
when he found an ant in Anthony.

Since he had found an ant in his name,
Anthony wondered
if he could find ants in other things.

So he searched all over his room.
He did not find an ant in a pair of pajamas,
or an ant in a goldfish bowl,
or an ant in a chest of drawers.

But he kept looking,
and he found an ant in a plant.

He searched in his backyard.
He did not find an ant in a barbecue,
or an ant in a lawn sprinkler,
or an ant in a hammock.

But he found an ant in a radio antenna.

He searched in the city.
He did not find an ant in a skyscraper,
or an ant in a crowd,
or an ant in a traffic jam.

He found an ant in a fire hydrant.

He searched the circus.
He did not find an ant in a flying trapeze,
or an ant in a clown,
or an ant in a bag of peanuts.

But he found an ant in an elephant.

He was getting hungry,
so he searched a fruit stand.
He did not find an ant in a banana,
or an ant in a piece of watermelon,
or an ant in a tangerine.

Surprise!
He found an ant in a cantaloupe.

He searched the zoo, too.
He did not find an ant in a panda bear,
or an ant in an armadillo,
or an ant in a kangaroo.

Instead, he found an ant in a panther.

He searched a haunted house.
He did not find an ant in a spiderweb,
or an ant in a skeleton,
or an ant in a bat.

Don't be scared.
He found an ant in a phantom.

He went to the library
and searched through some fairy tales.
He did not find an ant in a dragon,
or an ant in a knight in shining armor,
or an ant in a magic beanstalk.

He found an ant in a giant.

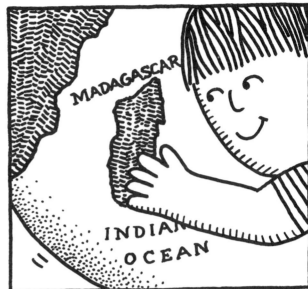

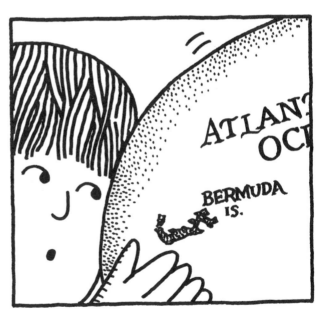

He searched around the globe.
He did not find an ant in Madagascar,
or an ant in Australia,
or an ant in Bermuda.

Of all places,
he found an ant in the Atlantic.

He searched the African jungle.
He did not find an ant in a crocodile,
or an ant in a hippopotamus,
or an ant in a ten-foot python.

But he did find an ant in an antelope.

He searched the North Pole.
He did not find an ant in a snowball,
or an ant in an explorer,
or an ant in a team of reindeer.

Of course, he found an ant in Santa.

He searched among all kinds of shapes.
He did not find an ant in a rectangle,
or an ant in a circle,
or an ant in an octagon.

But he looked some more,
and he found an ant in a slant.

Anthony was very tired
after finding so many ants,
so he sat down on the grass to rest.

Without looking for them,
he found ants in his pants.

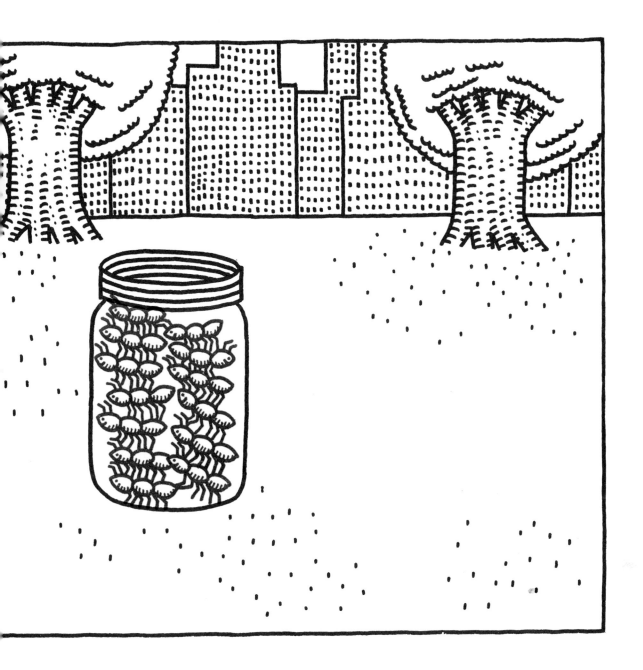

He had found enough ants for one day,
he thought,
so he ran home that instant.

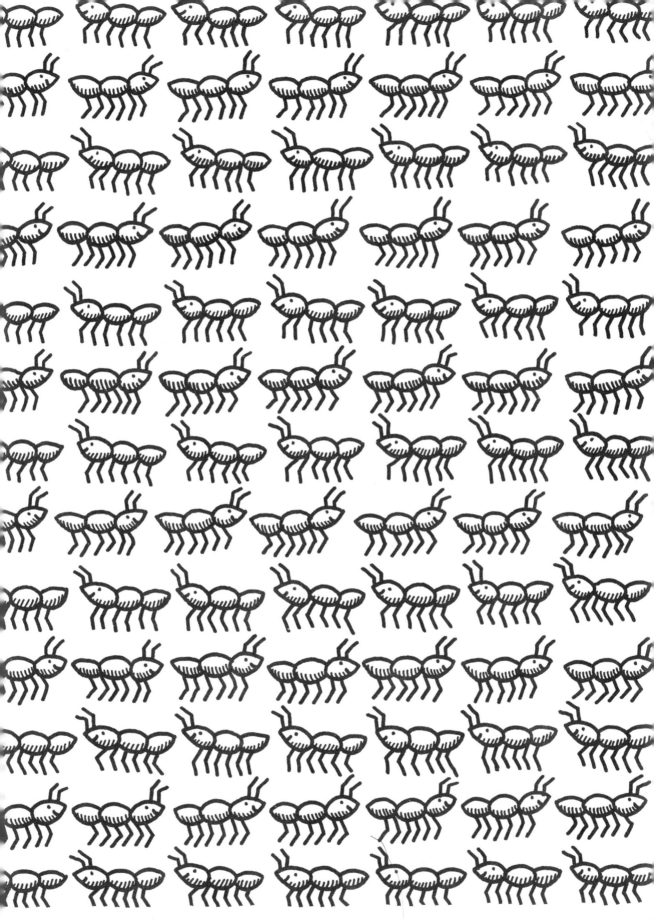